D0605257

You'll Be Sorry

by Josh Schneider

Clarion Books ⚜ New York

Clarion Books
a Houghton Mifflin Company imprint
215 Park Avenue South, New York, NY 10003
Copyright © 2007 by Josh Schneider

The illustrations were executed in watercolor and pen and ink.
The text was set in 22-point Baskerville.

www.clarionbooks.com

Printed in Singapore

Library of Congress Cataloging-in-Publication Data
Schneider, Josh, 1980–
You'll be sorry / by Josh Schneider.
p. cm.
Summary: Young Samantha does not believe her parents when they tell her to stop hitting her brother
or she will be sorry, but she soon learns just how right they are when his tears flood their entire town.
ISBN-13: 978-0-618-81932-4
ISBN-10: 0-618-81932-0
[1. Behavior—Fiction. 2. Brothers and sisters—Fiction. 3. Floods—Fiction.] I. Title.
II. Title: You will be sorry.
PZ7.S36335You 2007
[E]—dc22   2006033150

TWP 10 9 8 7 6 5 4 3 2 1

This book is dedicated to my two brothers,
for not being its inspiration.

"Don't hit your brother, or you'll be sorry," said Samantha's parents. But Samantha liked to hit her brother and did not think she'd be sorry. She thought she would be very sorry *not* to hit him.

So she hit him.

And he started crying. He would not stop. The carpets got all wet.

"Now you've done it," said Samantha's parents, and they went to get the family galoshes.

Samantha's brother cried and cried.
He cried buckets. The house was filling
up. Samantha's parents went to dig the
family rowboat out of the garage.

Samantha began to worry. The house had flooded, and the street had flooded, and her brother was still crying. Buckets.

Samantha's soccer game was canceled.

By dinnertime, Samantha's brother still had
not stopped crying, so they rowed over to
the supermarket and went fishing.
Samantha's father caught an orange, and
Samantha caught a box of soggy crackers.

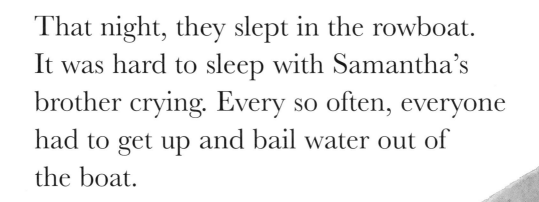

That night, they slept in the rowboat.
It was hard to sleep with Samantha's
brother crying. Every so often, everyone
had to get up and bail water out of
the boat.

Samantha woke up cold and wet. She was beginning to be sorry.

There was no school that day because of the flooding, but Samantha could not enjoy it. She was too sorry.

Her parents were ignoring her. Her mother had a headache from all the crying, and her father was crabby because he had missed his favorite television program. Still her brother was crying.

He looked so sad.

After a lunch of soggy crackers,
Samantha went over to her brother
and put her arm around him.

"I'm sorry I hit you," she apologized.

He sniffled.
Samantha dried his eyes.

They rowed back home.

29

"Don't pinch your brother, or you'll be sorry," said Samantha's parents. Samantha wanted very badly to pinch her brother . . . but she didn't do it.

Because she knew she would be.